The Perfect Gymnast

Michele Martin Bossley

James Lorimer & Company, Publishers
Toronto, 1996

James Lorimer & Company Ltd. acknowledges with thanks the support of the Canada Council and the Ontario Arts Council in the development of writing and publishing in Canada.

Cover illustration: Daniel Shelton

Canada Cataloguing in Publication Data

Bossley, Michele Martin
    The perfect gymnast

(Sports stories)
ISBN 1-55028-511-4 (bound)
ISBN 1-55028-510-6 (pbk.)

I. Title. II. Series: Sports stories (Toronto, Ont.)

PS8553.O77P47 1996 jC813'.54 C96-930147-2
PZ7.B67Pe 1996

James Lorimer & Company Ltd., Publishers
35 Britain Street
Toronto, Ontario
M5A 1R7

Printed and bound in Canada

Contents

Acknowledgements

Special thanks are due to Donna Cope and Shondi Bohne for their excellent suggestions regarding the sport of gymnastics; to Lisa Jefferies-Smith, head coach of the Women's Gymnastics program at the University of Calgary, for reading and checking this manuscript for accuracy prior to publication, for allowing me to sit in on gymnastic practices, and for her enthusiasm and advice; to Dr. Henry Koopmans of the Department of Psychology at the University of Calgary for his comments on eating disorders; to Tina Chan, for her helpful suggestions; to Laura Ellis for copyediting the manuscript; and to my editor Diane Young, for her insight and skill, both of which helped shape this story.

1

A Boiled Tomato with Hair

"Abigail Berkowski, what the heck do you think you're doing?"

I cringed. In addition to having my full name bellowed for all the neighbourhood to hear, I knew for absolute certain that Mrs. Spielini wasn't going to listen to my excuse.

I stood up. "I was just ..."

Mrs. Spielini leaned over her porch railing and pointed at my muddy sneakers. "Get your feet out of my garden! You're mashing my oregano plants."

I retreated to the sidewalk. "But my basketball ..."

Mrs. Spielini's eyes widened behind her bifocals. "You mean your basketball went crashing through here too?"

I nodded.

Mrs. Spielini moaned. "Why don't you just hire a bulldozer, Abby? Save yourself the trouble."

I tried not to smile. "Can I get it if I'm very careful?"

"No! You stay right there. I'll get it. Where did it go?"

"Under your porch."

I couldn't help grinning as Mrs. Spielini wiggled her bulky, blue-jeaned rear end and squeezed under the porch. She squashed a few parsley plants herself and knelt on the rosemary bush.

"Here." She bounced the dusty ball to me and shook a pile of cobwebs from her short grey hair. She looked at the bruised remains of her herb garden. "And don't stomp in my garden."

"I won't," I promised.

Mrs. Spielini's face relaxed into a smile. "Good. How about a piece of fresh zucchini bread? I just pulled a loaf out of the oven."

"Sure," I said.

Mrs. Spielini is my next-door neighbour and the first friend I've made in my new neighbourhood. In spite of her hollering about her herb plants (I've squashed them three times this week), she's really nice. She's energetic, loves gardening, racquetball, and yoga, and she makes the best zucchini bread I've ever tasted.

Mrs. Spielini sliced the still-warm loaf, slathered the pieces with butter, and set them on the well-worn kitchen table. I poured two glasses of iced tea.

"There," Mrs. Spielini said. "Now that's a snack!" She sat down in the chair beside me.

"So, Abby," she leaned back comfortably in her chair, "why aren't you out making friends with the girls down the street? The Kendrick sisters, now they're nice girls. And there's another one about your age ... twelve or so ... around the corner. Hmmm ... Tammy, no ... Tabitha Taylor, I think. She looks like a friendly kid."

I avoided her eyes, and the zucchini bread suddenly turned dry on my tongue. "I just haven't had much time, with moving and everything."

"Nonsense," Mrs. Spielini said briskly. "You've had time to bounce your basketball and stomp on my garden. You just haven't made time."

I swallowed carefully. "I guess."

"Abby," Mrs. Spielini leaned forward and patted my hand. "You've got to get out there and make some friends. It's not good to be alone so much."

"I'm not alone," I said. "I have my mom and dad, and I've met you."

"But you need friends your own age. An old lady like me can't get out and do much in the way of skateboarding."

"I hate skateboarding," I muttered. "Besides, you play racquetball and everything."

Mrs. Spielini threw up her hands. "You know what I mean, Abby."

"Yeah, I know," I said. "I …"

"Abby! Aaabbbyy! Where are you?" Through the kitchen window I could see my mother standing on our front lawn in her navy pinstriped suit and high heels, bellowing. I groaned inwardly.

"I'd better go," I said, getting up. I waved goodbye as I let the screen door swing shut behind me and ran over to my mother. "Mom!" I hissed. "Do you have to let the whole neighbourhood hear? Couldn't you just knock on the door?"

My mother ignored me. "Honey, I've asked you before to leave a note when you visit Mrs. Spielini, so I know where you are. For all I know, you could be anywhere."

"Yeah, but —"

"And anyway, I have some really exciting news." Mom plucked a bundle of flyers from the mailbox and opened our front door. She tossed the flyers on the stack of newspapers for the recycling bin, kicked off her shoes, and wriggled out of her suit jacket. "Oh, that feels better," she said. "I can't wait to get into some sweats."

"So what's your exciting news?" I pressed. "Did you win a case already?" My mother is a corporate lawyer, and since we just moved to Calgary from Edmonton, she's in a new firm. Sometimes she goes to court when companies are suing each other.

"No, better than that."

I followed her upstairs into my parents' bedroom. "Well, what?"

Mom sat down on the edge of the bed and began unclipping her gold-coloured earrings. "Well," she said. "I talked to a woman at work, and she said her daughter just loved this when she was in seventh grade, and I thought with you having such a hard time getting to know the kids in your class, it would just be perfect."

"What would be perfect?" I couldn't keep the alarm out of my voice.

"Now don't worry," Mom winced as the earring came loose and the clip caught in her dark hair. "It'll be so much fun."

"What is it?" I demanded.

"I signed you up for gymnastics. You start next week."

I shrieked.

"Abby, calm down." Mom gave me a disgusted look.

"Gymnastics! How could you do this to me? You know I'm a total klutz!" I panicked.

"Abby, you're not a klutz. You just don't have much confidence in yourself. Something like this is perfect for you."

Tears welled up in my eyes. "But I won't know anybody. Everyone will think I'm a loser, Mom. Please, don't make me go!"

"Abby, stop being silly. You're going, and that's the end of it." Mom hung her suit jacket in the closet and plucked her bathrobe from its hook. "I'm taking a shower before dinner."

She left me sitting on the edge of the bed, my sweaty hands clamped onto the soft quilt. I felt so angry I wanted to scream, so scared I wanted to cry. How could my own mother do something so horrible?

It's not that I hate gymnastics or anything. In fact, it's pretty interesting to watch. But I am absolutely the biggest geek that ever lived when I have to talk or perform in front of other people. I get paralyzed. My voice squeaks and I say dumb things. My feet and hands seem huge. I trip over things and my face gets so red and sweaty, I look like a boiled tomato with hair.

My mother knows this. And in spite of it, she keeps insisting that I need to be with kids more, make new friends, get more self-confidence. She thinks that I'll outgrow my clumsiness.

I doubt it. For as long as I can remember, I've always been scared and awkward around people I don't know.

My best friend in Edmonton was different. She was friendly and funny and she didn't care that I was shy. Elise made things easy when I met her in kindergarten. She just walked up to me and said, "Want to share my cookies? I don't like oatmeal."

I did like oatmeal cookies, and it didn't take very long before I liked Elise. We had a lot of fun together, until my family moved.

I really wished we hadn't left Edmonton. Even though I didn't have lots of friends in my old school, everybody knew I was shy, and they didn't make a big deal out of it.

The spray from the shower made a soft pattering against the glass doors, and I could smell the steamy scent of strawberry soap. I flopped back against the pile of designer pillows and heaved a gusty sigh.

Once Mom made up her mind, it was next to impossible to change it, even if I could get Dad on my side, which was unlikely. My dad travels a lot on business, so he's not here very often to stick up for me. Plus, Dad is almost as pushy as Mom about becoming a people person. He says I'll become antisocial if I'm not careful.

What's so wrong with wanting to be alone, for pete's sake?

2

First Time in the Gym

I swallowed very hard and reached for the car door handle. Mom patted my shoulder and smiled.

"Have fun, honey," she said encouragingly.

I didn't answer. I just pulled my nylon gym bag out from under the seat, opened the car door, and stepped out onto the sidewalk. Mom leaned across the passenger seat.

"Remember, wait in the lobby for me after your lesson."

I nodded. I was afraid to speak, in case the baseball-sized lump in my throat got in the way and made my voice sound weird. Instead of driving away, Mom let the car idle by the curb, waiting until I was safely inside.

I walked slowly up to the steps, dragged my feet to the top, and eyed the glass door with the words, "Briar Park Gymnastics Club" painted across the top. I wished I could stall for a few more minutes, but I could tell Mom was getting impatient. I looked back.

"Go on!" Mom gestured toward the door. I resisted the impulse to stick out my tongue, shoved the door open, and stepped inside.

The air smelled like floor wax and chalk dust. The linoleum in the reception area was old and beginning to curl at the corners, but someone had laid some colourful woven rugs down. The walls were freshly painted and hung with pictures, mostly posters of gymnasts with their bodies contorted into unbelievable positions. I wondered if anyone would expect me to do stuff like that.

A young woman dressed in black tights and a green T-shirt smudged with white dust came out from one of the locker rooms and paused beside the reception desk. She raked her fingers through her short, red-brown hair, and her hazel eyes regarded me with interest. "Hi," she said. "Are you new?"

I gulped and nodded.

"Okay, well, you can start by telling me your name." She gave me a friendly smile.

"Um. Abby. Abby Berkowski," I said.

"Okay, Abby. Let me find out what class you're in." She shuffled through the mass of papers on the desk and came up with a notebook. "You're in our beginners' class for older kids," she said. "Well, that's nice, because that's the class I coach today." She smiled again. "I'm Pam. I hope you'll have fun."

"Me too," I mumbled.

"Do you have a leotard or shorts to change into?"

"What do most kids wear?" I asked, immediately alarmed. Suppose Mom had bought the wrong thing?

"In beginners, usually leotards, I guess. But shorts are okay to start off with. All the advanced kids wear leotards, so the coaches can watch their body alignment." Pam shrugged as if she thought it wasn't important.

I knew better and breathed a sigh of relief. Mom had bought me a blue leotard with matching cotton leggings.

"All right then," Pam said. "Go get changed, put your hair up in a ponytail, and meet me on the red mats in the far corner of the gym." She gave me yet another encouraging smile and pointed me in the direction of the girls' locker room.

I took a deep breath and went in. A bunch of girls were already there, chattering and giggling as they scattered sneakers, underwear, and gym bags all over the floor. Everyone fell silent and stared as I walked in.

My mouth suddenly felt like it was coated with peanut butter, and any words were permanently stuck. I looked down at my feet and felt my face get hot. My neck began to itch under my jacket collar.

I set my bag down carefully on the floor in an empty spot in the corner and began to get changed. The silence was awful, but soon everyone forgot about me, and the teasing and laughter began again.

I slid into my leotard and leggings, thankful that I didn't stand out. Most of the girls wore something similar, in a wide variety of colours. I swept my long, light brown hair into a ponytail, secured it with a blue scrunchie, and checked myself quickly in the mirror. My eyes, normally light blue, looked wide and dark with nervousness. My skin was pasty pale and every freckle on my nose stood out. I grimaced and turned away, tossing my clothes into a locker. My bare feet felt cold on the tiled floor.

I knew Pam was waiting for me, but I couldn't bring myself to walk past all those girls. I hung back, pretending to fiddle with my hair until the locker room emptied, and then I ventured out to the gym.

It was huge — bright and spacious and airy. I stopped and stared. A large pail of chalk stood by the wall near the uneven bars, and the wood floor felt gritty from the chalk dust. The sight of the bars, balance beam, and vault — and the gymnasts who were flying and twisting over them — made my jaw drop in awe. Near me, a trampoline was set into a pit, so that it was level with the gym floor. Past the trampoline, the pit was filled with a tumbled mass of spongy foam blocks.

A girl was practising some kind of flip on the trampoline. Laughing, she catapulted off and plunged into the foam blocks. I watched her clamber out, completely unhurt, and get ready for another try.

"Abby, over here!" Pam waved from the red mats in the corner. A group of girls was already seated around her. Reluctantly, I trudged over to join them and edged in beside a few kids I recognized from my class at school. I glanced around the group and was relieved to find that everyone was wearing a similar outfit to mine and had their hair pulled back in braids or ponytails, except for one girl, whose dark hair was cut short. So far, it was easy for me to blend in.

"Okay, everybody," Pam said, beaming at all of us with her wide smile. "Welcome to our beginners' class. We divide our beginners into age categories, so you get to make friends with other kids your age, and we don't have you older guys practising with the kindergarten kids."

I wondered if that was supposed to make this whole thing less humiliating. After all, even I knew that most very good gymnasts start when they're really young. Twelve is old. I squirmed, realizing that there were probably seven and eight year olds in this club who could make me look like a huge idiot.

"So today we'll just get started on some basic gymnastic skills and let you try out the apparatus, so it doesn't seem so scary, okay?" Pam was still smiling.

It was a relief that she was so friendly. I hoped she wouldn't hold it against me when I completely messed up in front of the other girls.

"Let's start by jogging around the edge of the mats. Please run on the mat, not the floor. It's easier on your knees."

The mats were stuck together to form a large square area, and Pam led us through six laps at a brisk pace. I was panting when we were done.

"Next, we stretch out," Pam said. "This is very important, so please make sure you always do a good job on every stretch. It's very easy to pull a muscle if you haven't stretched properly."

We went through a long series of stretches. By the time we were halfway through, I felt like my body was an elastic band. Shoulder, wrist, neck, torso, and practically a million leg stretches were all part of the program. I've always been really flexible, and I found that I could actually do most of the stretches better than everyone else in my class, including getting all the way down in the splits on both legs.

Pam was very impressed. "Good for you," she encouraged.

Flexibility was something I had always taken for granted, just like my shorter-than-average height and stick-straight brown hair. I felt embarrassed and pleased at the same time. I hadn't expected to be good at anything.

"All right, let's get started on some floor exercises," Pam said. "I'm sure you've all done forward rolls and backward rolls before, but we're going to practise them today."

"You mean somersaults?" asked one girl.

"No. A somersault, or salto in gymnastics, is an aerial roll, where you don't touch the ground."

"Oh," the girl said in a small voice. I knew how she felt and gulped nervously.

Pam showed us how to do the rolls, starting and ending in a standing position. She made them look a lot more graceful than the tumbling around in the backyard I used to do. Then we tried cartwheels, which weren't too hard, but Pam demanded that we work on proper form. After that Pam spotted us for handstands. She explained that "spotting" is when your coach stands by to help you perform a skill and catches you if you fall.

"Good work, girls," Pam congratulated us at the end of the floor workout. "Now we get to move on to the apparatus for the last twenty minutes." She grinned as she saw several faces go pale, mine included.

"Don't worry. We won't be trying anything fancy."

And we didn't. On the uneven bars, Pam explained about handgrips and some of the different moves we'd eventually work on. Then she helped each of us jump up to the low bar and balance on our hips, just to see how it felt to be up there.

She did pretty much the same thing on the balance beam. We practised walking on it, while Pam talked about learning jumps and dismounts.

"And this," Pam said, moving to the last station, "is the vault." She touched a heavy piece of equipment that looked like a sawhorse with a fat leather pillow glued to the top. "This is the horse, and this is the beatboard." She gestured to the wooden apparatus on the floor in front of the horse.

My stomach clenched itself into knots when I thought about how I was going to have to bounce off the beatboard without tangling myself up on the horse.

Pam stepped onto the beatboard and began to bounce on the high edge, her hands resting on the horse. "This is the take-off point," she said. "For today we're just going to practise using the beatboard and landing on the horse. The idea is to hit a smooth, fast stride as you run, land on the beatboard at the take-off point, and get lots of power to propel you onto the horse. I'll show you so you get the idea."

Pam backed off down the gym. She rocked back and forth on her toes for a minute, then began to run. Her legs pumped up and down in a blur, and the beatboard made a popping noise like a cork coming out of a bottle as she hit the take-off point. She sailed over the horse, her hands hardly touching the vault, her legs tucked high into her chest. She landed on the thick, soft mat on the other side of the horse, stretched her hands above her head, and lifted her chin. She turned to face us.

"That's called a squat vault. Notice how I finished it? Always extend your arms, don't slouch, and try to look as graceful as possible," Pam said. "You guys don't have to try a squat vault, just try to land on the horse. Okay?"

I felt sick. Graceful? Me? Hah!

"Is everybody ready to try it?" Pam asked. Most of the girls looked enthusiastic and nervous at the same time. I tried to hide behind everybody and wished I could somehow escape.

"All right. Head down to the end then, and I'll be waiting to catch you if you fall off the horse. Just try your best."

I dragged my feet behind the group and tried to worm my way to the back. Unfortunately, nobody seemed eager to be the first one to blast down the runway and leap onto that horse, which looked bigger by the minute.

"Come on, you guys," Pam called. "We don't have all day! It doesn't matter who goes first."

The group shuffled around, but still no one volunteered to start.

"Okay!" Pam shouted. "Line up. Abby, how about you trying it first?"

I thought I would choke. Pam smiled from her position at the horse.

"Don't be scared. I'll help you."

The other girls waited for me to go. I wished I could run back to the locker room, out of the gym, and disappear forever.

But there was no way out. I took a deep breath and rocked back and forth a little on my toes, the way Pam had shown us. Then I ran toward the beatboard. The horse loomed larger every instant.

My breath caught in my throat and I was about to lurch to a panicked stop when my big toe caught on the edge of the beatboard and I had to leap to keep from stumbling. I landed with all my weight on the take-off point and suddenly I was flying. I stretched my hands toward the horse and instinctively tucked my legs up out of the way. I sailed over the horse, pushed my legs through and landed, stunned, on the soft mat.

"Excellent!" Pam cried. "Look proud, Abby. Extend your arms and finish the vault properly."

I felt silly, but I raised my arms and lifted my chin before I stepped off the mat.

"Good girl," Pam said. She squeezed my shoulder as I walked past. "Have you ever tried vaulting before?"

I shook my head.

"Then you're a natural," she smiled.

I nearly floated back to the group of girls waiting to try their turn at the vault.

"Nice," one girl commented. "How did you do it?"

"Uh ... well ... just lucky, I guess," I whispered truthfully.

"Hmmm," the girl looked me up and down, then turned to the others. "Well, maybe vaulting's not so hard, then."

"Yeah," said another.

But each one of them tried, and the best anyone could do was bounce weakly from the beatboard and plop onto the horse. A flicker of pride warmed me, and when it was my turn again, I was determined to do another squat vault, even better than the first.

I sprinted down the runway and hit the beatboard with all my strength. It gave a muffled pop, and this time I headed straight for the horse, not over it. Scared, I thrust out my hands and tried to push myself up before I smashed right into it.

Pam's hands grabbed my waist. "Tuck, Abby!"

I pulled my legs in and pushed with my arms. I landed unsteadily on top of the horse.

"Good," Pam said.

I blinked and exhaled slowly. "I nearly killed myself," I gasped.

"That's what I'm here for." Pam winked. "To make sure that you don't."

I managed a wobbly grin.

Pam glanced at the clock. "We won't have time for you to try another vault today, so why don't you just relax and stretch out over there until the rest of the class is done?" she suggested, pointing to a group of small practice mats in the corner.

"Okay." I wandered over to the mats and flopped down, relieved to be away from the group for a while. As I worked on some legs stretches, I watched the other gymnasts. Some of them were very good, especially compared to my class. After our simple vault and floor exercises, I realized how difficult those skills must be.

I watched one girl in particular. She had a small frame, a pixie face, and a stiffly braided black pigtail. She flew and twisted over the uneven bars as if gravity didn't exist. She flung her tightly muscled body high into the air, tucked and spun herself into a human pretzel, and then miraculously straightened out to plant her feet firmly on the mat.

"She's good, isn't she?" Pam said, suddenly showing up at my elbow.

"Yes," I answered, awestruck. "Who is she?"

"Hilary Chen. She's working toward Junior Nationals this year."

"How old is she?" I wondered.

"She's thirteen."

"Oh." I found that hard to believe. I would have guessed that she was ten, or maybe eleven.

Pam clapped me on the shoulder. "Anyway, class is over. You did a great job today, Abby. You were the only one who managed that vault. You should be proud."

I gave Pam a smile. "Thanks."

"See you on Thursday."

"Okay." I loped toward the locker room. I did feel proud. I'd lived through one gymnastics class without causing a world disaster. Maybe it wasn't going to be so horrible after all. But I wasn't going to tell my mother that.

3

Out of the Spotlight

I traced my pencil along the carved initials in my desk and stifled a yawn. Mr. Kramer, who was both my Language Arts and homeroom teacher, gave a weary sigh.

"Could someone check the calendar?" he said. "I could have sworn the Halloween dance was still two weeks away, but it seems that someone's replaced my class with a bunch of zombies." Mr. Kramer glanced around the room. "Come on, people! I know memorizing this stuff isn't easy, but let's get it together, okay?"

The class shuffled and groaned.

Dr. Alfred Sponnick Junior High wasn't much different from my old school. We changed classes every forty minutes, and we were allowed to eat lunch outside when it was nice. Everyone still gave teachers, especially substitutes, a hard time when they were bored.

I sat up and began copying the grammar lesson off the blackboard. Verb, adverb, adjective, noun, preposition — the list went on endlessly. Bleah!

I don't mean to say that I don't like writing. In fact, I love to write. I just hate memorizing stuff for tests.

I kept scribbling definitions and phrases while Mr. Kramer talked, and I found myself thinking about gymnastics. I felt great when Pam congratulated me on my vault. I wondered if I could do it again.

Mr. Kramer stepped back to the blackboard and erased it. "Okay, notebooks closed. Time for Language Arts *Jeopardy*. Each row is a team — that gives us six teams."

He wrote the numbers one through six on the board. I was on team two.

"Answer in the form of a question. The first person to give a correct answer gets a point for their team. Ready? Okay. Give me the grammatical term for an action word. Anyone?"

Everyone looked blank.

Verb, I thought anxiously. Come on, team two! I ached to give the answer, but I just couldn't bring myself to shout it out in front of the class.

"Whhhaaannk! Sorry. Time's up. The answer is, 'what is a verb?' Next — the punctuation used when someone is speaking aloud."

Oh, man! I squirmed. Quotation marks! Someone say quotation marks!

Allyson Mills from team six put up her hand.

"Allyson?" Mr. Kramer pointed.

"What are quotation marks?"

"Bingo!" Mr. Kramer marked down a point. "Next — the word used to describe anything that is a person, place, or thing."

That is so easy! A noun! Why didn't anyone on our team know that? I clenched my hands.

I grew more frustrated as each team received at least one point, and team two stayed at zero.

"Okay, last one." Mr. Kramer straightened his glasses. "The grammatical term for a word that connects phrases, sentences, or clauses."

The class was silent. The seconds ticked by, and I couldn't stand it any more.

My hand shot into the air, just as Mr. Kramer yelled.

"Whhhaan — hold everything! Abby?" Mr. Kramer looked surprised, since I hadn't yet said one word in class.

"What is a conjunction?" I said.

Mr. Kramer beamed. "Correct!" he said. "That means team two is saved from utter disgrace by Abby Berkowski."

The class giggled, and team two looked embarrassed.

I chewed on a hangnail and felt the familiar blush creep up my neck into my face. I just couldn't help it. Being the centre of attention made me painfully uncomfortable. I wished I hadn't opened my mouth.

Soon the class lost interest in me, and Mr. Kramer went on with his discussion. I didn't pay much attention, until he began talking about a talent contest.

"... so, because the school's budget won't be enough to cover all the renovations we'd like for the library expansion, this year we'll be holding our first annual school talent show in December, just before Christmas vacation. We hope the show will help raise some extra funds."

"What talent?" smirked Will Bryant. Will was the type of kid who always looked for attention, even if it meant getting in trouble. He was tall and gangly, with a round freckled face that always seemed ready to laugh.

Mr. Kramer answered mildly. "You might be surprised, Will." He fixed all of us with an encouraging grin. "And if any of you enter the writing competition, I'll put it toward your final grade."

"Great," Will muttered.

Mr. Kramer ignored him. "The categories are drama, writing, music, and entertainment. The top five in each category will be chosen to perform in the talent show, and a special achievement award will be presented to first place winners at the show."

I could see many pairs of eyes gleaming. Allyson Mills was practically licking her lips at the mention of an award given before an adoring audience.

There was no way I'd enter that contest. You couldn't get me up on that stage for all the money in the world. Not a chance. I slouched down in my seat.

"Okay, kids, start thinking about what you'd like to do. Here's an info sheet to take home. The tryout and submission deadlines are listed, as well as what teacher to see. I'm in charge of the writing competition." Mr. Kramer began passing out the papers. "Don't forget, everyone is encouraged to join up."

I took the info sheet reluctantly and stuffed it in my math textbook. The sheet was photocopied on bright green paper, and it was pretty hard to ignore. I planned to throw it in the garbage as soon as I got home.

4

Meeting Hilary

Thursday after school, Mom dropped me off at the gym again. I wasn't as nervous as the first time, but I still wasn't convinced that this class was a good idea.

I mean, the other girls in my class didn't seem very friendly. After all, no one tried to talk to me. What if I didn't make any friends? What if no one liked me? I wished I could just open my mouth and have some magically cool conversation come pouring out. If only people could see what I was like inside.

I took a deep breath before I walked into the locker room, determined to smile and act normal. As soon as I stepped inside, the girl who had talked to me after my vault last class eyed me, turned away, and giggled to her best friend. My face burned. What was she saying? What was so funny?

I swallowed all my good intentions and got changed without looking or smiling at anyone. I edged through the crowd as inconspicuously as possible and shrank into a corner of the gym to stretch before my lesson.

Hilary Chen was practising her floor routine with Pam. Pam still had a cheerful expression on her face, but I could see from her look of concentration that she demanded a lot more of Hilary than she did of my class. Hilary was working on a skill that sent her twisting and flipping over and over into the air. I got chills just watching her. Suppose she messed up and fell? Ouch!

And Hilary did mess up, too. Once she didn't get enough momentum and managed only one and a half turns before plummeting to the mat. Pam reached for her and helped slow her fall, but Hilary still ended up on her rear end.

"Okay?" Pam asked, as Hilary rose to her feet. Hilary nodded, rubbed her bruised hip, and trotted back to the end of the mat to try again.

"Start from the dance moves before your last tumbling line," Pam said.

Hilary executed some spins and gliding steps on the balls of her feet, then lifted her back leg into an unbelievably high arabesque and held it for a moment. I wondered how she managed to make everything she did look effortless and graceful.

She swung around into position to start her run for the round-off, which is like a cartwheel that's cut off in the middle, when both feet are thrust down at once. Gymnasts often use round-offs to build the momentum they need for other moves.

Hilary's small body was so quick and energized it reminded me of a coiled spring. She flew through the air, she snapped into the round-off and sprang into a back handspring. *Whap, whap, whap!* She nailed two handsprings in a row and bounded high into the air for a double back pike.

Hilary's toes stretched for the mat. *Whump!* She landed steadily and extended her arms.

"Yes!" yelled Pam exultantly. "That's it!" She clapped Hilary on the shoulder.

Hilary smiled and wiped the sweat off her forehead with the sleeve of her red leotard. "Can I get a drink and stretch a bit before I go to bars with Carlo?" she asked.

Pam glanced at her watch. "Okay, but don't get too cooled off. You have about five minutes."

Hilary took a quick drink from the fountain, walked over to the mats where I was stretching and plopped down beside me.

"Some wipeout, huh?" she said, grinning. "I saw you watching."

"Some terrific ending," I blurted. "That last flip was fantastic."

Hilary smiled. "I'm Hilary Chen. Who are you?"

"Abby Berkowski. I'm in the beginners' class." I felt suddenly shy.

Hilary began to stretch out her hips. "New, huh? Well, it's a fun sport. Competitive, though." She smiled again.

I nodded. "Yeah."

Hilary eyed me up and down, and I felt self-conscious and awkward, like I was sitting in my underwear.

"You know, Abby," she said. "You have a really good body for gymnastics. You're small, and you look strong. Are you flexible?"

I nodded. "Yeah. I guess so."

Hilary smiled again. "Well, keep practising. Maybe someday we'll compete together!"

I laughed. That was pretty far-fetched, and I knew it. But it was still nice of Hilary to say it.

She stood up abruptly. "I have to go. Carlo just came in, and he throws a fit if I keep him waiting." She trotted off to the uneven bars, where the coach I saw her working with during my last class was frowning impatiently.

The rest of my class had wandered into the gym, and Pam was waving me over to the floor section.

"Okay," she cried. "Everybody remember the stretching drill?"

A chorus of groans assured her that we did. My muscles were already warm, so the stretches were even easier than before. On the next mat, a blond girl I recognized from my class at school looked at me enviously.

"I wish I could do the splits like that," she said. "Are you in ballet or something?"

I shook my head. "No. I just have loose muscles, I guess."

"Lucky," she said. Her rosy face widened into a dimpled grin, and she tossed her curly ponytail back over one shoulder. "Not me." Her own plump legs were pressed stiffly into the splits, but her thighs were still at least a foot off the floor.

I shrugged and wished I could think of something else to say. If only I could make a friend in my class! "Are ... are you ... have you ever done gymnastics before?" I stammered, and then immediately wanted to kick myself. Of course she hadn't. If she had, why would she be in the beginners' class?

"Nope," the girl said cheerfully. "My mom thinks I should get more exercise, so she signed me up for gymnastics and soccer, and told me I have to try out for at least one school sport this year. She says I watch too much TV."

"Mine says that too," I said. "About television, I mean."

The girl shook her head in exasperation. "Parents! They're all the same."

Pam clapped her hands for attention. "All right, girls! Let's go through the same floor exercises as last time."

This time the drill went faster. Pam began correcting us on form, reminding us to point our toes and keep our knees and elbows straight.

I found out that the blond girl who had talked to me was named Sophie, and she seemed to have a lot of friends. I wished I could be that popular. Instead I went through the floor exercises on my own, while everyone else talked and giggled as they practised.

"Okay everybody, pair up," Pam said. "I'm going to teach you how to spot each other in a handstand."

I swallowed with difficulty. In phys. ed. last year I could always count on Elise for a partner, but when you're a new kid, especially a shy new kid, you're always the one left over.

Pam didn't make a big deal out of it. She used me to show everyone else what to do, which meant that the whole class watched me try a handstand. Pam had a good chance to demonstrate spotting techniques, since I kept bungling it and tumbling to the mat because I was so nervous.

My cheeks burned. Then I glanced over to where Hilary was working on the bars. Her face held a look of total concentration. She didn't see me, or the other girls waiting for their turn. She didn't care who saw her mess up. She just tried again.

I held up my head. If Hilary didn't care, then I didn't either. Pam smiled encouragingly.

"Ready to try again?" she asked.

I nodded. Taking a deep breath, I tightened my body, planted my hands on the mat, and kicked my legs over my head.

"Tighten your bum and your stomach," Pam said, but she didn't reach to help me.

I squeezed every muscle and held the handstand for a few seconds before I swung my legs back down and stood up.

"Terrific!" Pam cried. "That was great!"

I glowed.

"Okay class, that's exactly what I want everybody to do. Go ahead and practise with your partners. Try and hold the handstand, keeping your legs straight and toes pointed. Spotters, be ready."

Pam turned to me. "Want to try again?"

I looked at Hilary, who was chalking her hands before she got back on the bars.

"Absolutely," I said.

5

Keeping It All Inside

Abby, 'no' is not an acceptable answer." My mother waved the bright green sheet of paper in the air. "Why on earth would you throw this away?"

I snatched it from her. "Why were you going through my garbage?" I demanded.

"I wasn't going through it, I was emptying it," Mom huffed.

I cursed myself for not having the sense to flush the contest information sheet down the toilet. Now I was really in for it.

"Look, Mom," I tried to be logical. "I don't have any musical or creative talent, you know I wouldn't be able to get up on stage, and I'm taking the stupid gymnastics classes like you forced me to, so why can't you just forget about it?" My logic was dissolving into irritation. I couldn't help it.

"Well, for starters, I haven't heard any complaints lately about gymnastics, so I have to conclude that you're enjoying it."

"Fat chance," I muttered. I refused to admit to her that it wasn't turning out to be so bad.

"And," Mom continued, ignoring me, "you used to take piano lessons. It would be nice to brush up on your skills."

"Mom!" I wailed. "That was four years ago! I absolutely refuse to get up in front of everyone at the tryouts and play 'Twinkle, Twinkle, Little Star.' You've got to be kidding me."

"Well then," Mom said, not to be deterred. "Why not recite a poem, or learn a monologue from a play or something?"

I pretended to gag.

"You certainly have enough dramatic talent," Mom said drily.

"No, Mother. Absolutely not. I refuse to take part in a contest that will force me to get up in front of the school and make a horse's rear end out of myself. Even if I don't get accepted into the top five, which I won't, I'd still be humiliated at the stupid tryouts. I'm not doing it. No way. And that's final." I folded my arms across my chest.

Mom sat down in the chair opposite me and looked at me silently for a few minutes. "Abby," she said softly. "You are such a terrific person. Why won't you let the world see it?"

I suddenly found myself blinking back tears.

"You have a whole host of talents. You're smart, you're loyal, you have a great sense of humour, you really care about people. If you would only try to develop one-tenth of those things …"

"That's not true," I blurted. "How can you even think that? I mean, I know you're my mother, but still …" I stopped before I started blubbering.

Mom's face twisted with sympathy. "Abby …" she reached for me and smothered me in a tight hug. I started to cry. I cried because I felt awkward and embarrassed and scared half the time. I cried because I missed Edmonton and Elise and my old school. I cried because I was tired of being too shy to make friends and worrying about what other people thought of me. I cried until I had used up all my tears, and then mopped my face and wiped my nose with the sleeve of my sweatshirt.

"Abby," Mom repeated, releasing me. "I'm going to tell you one of those stories you hate."

I grimaced. "The ones that begin, 'When I was your age'?"

"Yup." Mom smiled. "When I was your age, I was just like you."

I looked up in surprise.

"I was very shy, and I thought I was a nerd, and I could hardly open my mouth to anyone. If the teacher called on me in class, I would turn beet red from my forehead to my feet. I would stammer and stutter, even if I knew the answer, just because people were looking at me."

"So what happened?" I said. "You certainly don't have that problem now."

"No, I certainly don't. A successful lawyer may be many things, but shy isn't usually one of them."

"No kidding."

"Anyway, I grew up, I guess. I figured out that I really was smart, that I really could play sports, and that I really could talk without seeming like a nerd at all, once I learned to relax in front of other people." Mom flashed a wry grin. "Most people are too busy worrying about what you think of them."

I considered that. "Maybe."

"What I'm trying to say, Abby, is that I didn't want you to go through all that. I wanted you to try new things and become self-confident, so you wouldn't be afraid like I was. I've pushed you into things because I knew you were shy."

"Well, what's wrong with being shy?"

"Nothing, as long as it doesn't stop you from doing the things you want to do. For instance, if you weren't scared to get up on that stage, wouldn't it feel great to be picked for the talent contest?"

"I guess so," I said slowly. "Maybe."

"Well then, do you see how being shy has stopped you from doing something that you might otherwise really want to do?"

"Mom," I complained. "You're starting to sound like a lawyer."

"All right!" Mom grinned. "I'll shut up. Just promise me you'll think about entering the contest, okay?"

"Okay," I muttered. I felt better, but not enough to feel excited about the contest. I took the crumpled green sheet of paper reluctantly and examined it.

Music ... no. I wasn't going to try playing the piano in front of everyone. Drama ... forget it. Entertainment ... no way. That was as bad as drama. Writing ... hmmm.

The info sheet said that all writing submissions had to be an original story, essay, or poem. I didn't have to try out, just hand my essay in to Mr. Kramer. I liked to write anyway, and I'd get extra credit for Language Arts class.

The writing contest was a possibility.

6

Fitting In

"Hey, have you mastered that back tuck dismount off the beam yet?" Hilary teased. She brushed the loose chalk dust off her palms and gave me a friendly grin. Hilary was just starting her bar warm-up as I walked over to join my class.

"No, not yet," I joked. "But I'm working on it." Back tuck dismount! Like, really.

"Don't worry, you'll get it," Hilary said. "Pam'll have you doing aerials in no time."

"Hah." But I smiled at her. She made me feel confident, like I really could do a back tuck dismount someday if I worked at it.

I felt so good I found myself smiling at the rest of my class, too. Sophie noticed.

"Hey, you look happy," she said.

"Kind of," I admitted. "I feel like trying something new today."

"Well, you're in luck," Sophie said. "Pam just told us she's going to get us to work on back walkovers today."

"Great." For a change it didn't seem so scary to try something new, and that felt good.

Pam showed us a back walkover, which was definitely the most difficult floor skill we'd tried so far. You have to bend over backwards until your hands touch the floor, kick one leg over and push off with the other, and balance yourself in a handstand with your legs in the splits (or as close as you can get to the splits). Then you bring your legs down to the floor and stand up.

That takes muscles! No matter how hard I tried, I couldn't push off my legs hard enough. I kept collapsing.

Sophie offered to spot me, after Pam showed us how. Surprised and pleased, I let her, and before our time on the floor was up, I managed to do one wobbly back walkover all by myself.

"Yes!" Sophie cheered. The other girls in our class looked over, but they just smiled and went on working. I didn't feel embarrassed at all.

After class was over, I walked out with Sophie, and she included me in the conversation with her friends, just as if she had known me forever. We stopped to watch Hilary's group work on the balance beam with Pam, who coached them on floor and beam after she finished teaching our beginners' class. Carlo coached Hilary's group on bars and vault.

Hilary waved to me while she waited for her turn.

"I can't believe the stuff they can do," said Lisa, one of Sophie's friends.

"I know," Sophie said, awed. "They're amazing."

Hilary climbed up on the beam and began a series of leaps and turns. She wobbled and nearly fell.

"Hilary, concentrate!" yelled Pam.

Hilary nodded and her face took on the same intense, focused look I'd seen when she worked on the bars. Her turns became tighter and cleaner, her leaps higher. She paused at the end of the beam, pivoted, then launched herself into a round-off back handspring combination.

We let out an audible sigh of relief when she landed with both feet firmly on the beam. Hilary used a simple dismount, and her feet hit the thick cushiony mat at the end of the beam with a soft plop.

She passed by us on her way to the end of the line, as another girl began her turn. "Piece of cake," she murmured to me. I could tell she was joking, not bragging, by the goofy face she made when she said it.

"Are you friends with her?" Sophie asked when we were in the locker room getting changed.

"Yeah," I said, feeling important. "I mean, I just met her at the last practice, but we've been talking a lot."

"She's really good. Like the best in the club." Sophie sounded wistful.

"I know," I said.

Sophie shouldered her gym bag, and she and Lisa waved as they walked out. "See you," they called.

"Bye," I said, smiling.

As I shoved my feet into my sneakers, a sudden thought hit me. I actually liked gymnastics class. I had actually made friends. And, miracle of miracles, I didn't feel like the clumsiest kid in the class any more. Pam made it seem natural to make mistakes. She kept telling us to try again. Today every single person had messed up on something. Nobody was perfect.

And Hilary thought I could be good someday. Sophie wished she could do the splits like me. I was actually good at something!

I had never felt so terrific in my life.

***

At school the next day, I was struggling with my locker, which didn't seem to enjoy being stuffed with a gym bag, a knapsack, piles of textbooks and homework, my ski jacket, and gym shoes. As I was trying to cram everything in, I felt a tap on my shoulder. I gave the whole mess a good shove, slammed my locker door, and whirled around.

Hilary stood behind me. "Hi," she said. "Going for a world record?"

"Huh?"

She tapped my locker. "For how much stuff you can get in there."

I laughed. "No." I looked at her. She wore her hair loose at school, so it fell in a straight black curtain around her shoulders, and her flannel shirt and faded jeans were well worn. She had topped off her outfit with a pair of old hiking boots. If I didn't know better, I'd never guess that Hilary was a champion gymnast.

"Wow," I said. "I barely recognized you."

Hilary glanced at her clothes. "Yeah. I like to be comfortable, even if I look like a bag lady. Hey, I didn't know you went to my school."

"I just moved here at the beginning of September," I said. I shifted uncomfortably and willed myself not to blush. Why did I always feel so awkward at school? I felt fine with Hilary at the gym.

"So, do you want to eat lunch together, or something?" Hilary leaned against my locker door.

"Sure," I said eagerly.

"Great. Let's go."

For the first time I walked into the cafeteria without feeling like a leftover, unnecessary something. I had a friend, and that made all the difference.

"Where do you want to sit?" I asked.

Hilary wrinkled her nose at the hot-lunch counter, where the greasy smell of french fries and hot dogs and the spicy smell of day-old chili filled the air. "As far away from that as possible."

I sniffed and shrugged. It didn't seem so bad to me, but I wasn't about to argue. We found a table in the farthest corner and sat down.

I had brought a thick tuna sandwich, a juice box, carrot sticks, a pear, and chocolate-chip cookies. Hilary had brought a small container of diet yoghurt, a stalk of celery, an apple, and a stick of sugarless gum.

"Is that all you're having?" I asked.

Hilary nodded. "I want to keep my weight down." She sighed. "It's hard, though. I love french fries and cake and stuff."

"Yeah, me too." I eyed her lunch. It seemed awfully small, even for somebody as tiny as Hilary.

Hilary ate her celery and spooned a few mouthfuls of yoghurt into her mouth as I ate my lunch. When I was finished, she stood up, the yoghurt container still half full, her apple untouched.

"Want to go outside?" she asked. "We can sit out by the fence and watch the soccer practice before the bell. It's the girls' team versus the boys'."

"Okay," I said. "But don't you want to finish eating?"

Hilary glanced at her yoghurt. "No." She tossed it in a nearby trash can and stuffed the apple in the pocket of her jacket. "Come on. We'll miss the game if we don't hurry."

I followed her outside. We found a place where we could watch the soccer teams, and talked and giggled.

Hilary propped her elbows up on her knees and watched the soccer game with interest. "You know what, Abby," she said. "You could be a really good gymnast, if you wanted. You've improved so much already."

"Really?" I felt myself blush. "But I just started. I could never be as good as you."

Hilary smiled. "I've been in gymnastics since I was four. That's a long time." She paused. "You know, being a great gymnast is more important to me than anything else in the whole world. I can't describe how I feel when I compete. It's like this whole other part of me takes over, and I'm flying."

I wasn't sure what to say.

"That's why it's so hard when I can't do a skill I'm working on, like that stupid double back pike you saw last week. I need to do it on the beam, and I can barely do it on the floor. I've just got to nail it before the invitational competition in December," she sighed. "If I weighed less, I know the double back pike would be easier. I just know I'd get it for sure."

"I don't know, Hilary," I said doubtfully. "I don't think …"

"You know, Pam and Carlo have already talked about training me for the Olympic Trials, if I do well in the next year or so." Hilary's eyes lit up. "Oh Abby, if only I could go! My parents would be so proud, and I don't want to disappoint them. I want to be perfect. I just have to work hard."

"Wow." I felt awed.

"Yeah. But I have to be so tough on myself, or else I'll never make it." She groaned slightly, then relaxed and changed the subject. "So are you going to the Halloween dance on Friday?" she asked.

"Um … I don't know," I answered. "I'm not … well … I don't like dances very much."

"Oh, Abby, how come?" Hilary tore her gaze away from the game and looked at me in surprise. "They're so much fun! Especially Halloween! You get to wear neat costumes and you have to guess who everybody is. It's a blast! You've got to come."

"I don't know …" I hesitated.

"I'll help you with a costume, if you want," Hilary offered. "Come on, Abby, say you'll go. It'll be fun."

"Well," I wavered. "Okay."

"Great!" Hilary squeezed my arm.

7

The Halloween Dance

So, what do you think?" Hilary held up the two black bath towels she'd stitched together at the top edges, leaving just enough space for a head to fit through the top. "Is this hole big enough?" She slipped it over my head and looked at me.

I glanced in my bedroom mirror. One bath towel drooped across my chest, the other sagged against my back. They were held together by the seams on each of my shoulders. "Are you sure this is going to work?" I asked.

"Trust me," Hilary said confidently. "This is going to be great. Hold still while I stitch the sides. Then the whole thing won't be so floppy."

She basted up each side with big, loopy stitches in black thread. "The thread is easier to take out if you sew it big," Hilary explained. "Besides, this is faster."

"As long as it holds together," I said. I had horrible visions of the whole costume disintegrating in the middle of the dance.

"It will. Hold still." Hilary tied a knot just under my armpit and started on the other side. "Okay," she said finally. "You can take it off. We'll put the dots on now."

I pulled the towels carefully up over my head and pushed my static-charged hair back from my face. Hilary rapidly sewed the large dots cut from white felt onto the front towel.

"Put on my black turtleneck, Abby, and your black leggings," Hilary said. "I'm almost done."

My mom peeked around the door just as I was pulling the finished costume over my head. She burst out laughing.

I surveyed myself in the mirror. "I'm a domino!" I said, grinning.

"If that isn't clever!" Mom said. "Whose idea was it?"

"Hilary's," I said.

"Well, not really," Hilary laughed. "I saw this costume before in a magazine."

"Well, it looks super. I'm so glad you're going to the dance, Abs. You two'll have a lot of fun."

Hilary nodded enthusiastically, but I felt myself wilting inside. Costume or no costume, how was I supposed to talk to people and dance without making a fool out of myself?

Hilary pulled my hair to the nape of my neck and secured it with a black-and-white polka dotted scrunchie. "Perfect!" she said.

The costume was great. It was funny and original. But I'd still have to dance and talk and do all those things that I constantly bungle.

Hilary pulled on her hiking boots and I walked out to the sidewalk with her, still wearing my domino costume. Mrs. Spielini was digging in her flower beds, pulling out dead plants and wrapping her rose bushes in burlap sacks to protect them from the cold. She looked up, and her dirt-streaked face broke into a wide smile.

"Great costume, Abby!" she called. She struggled to her feet and pulled off her gardening gloves. "Going trick-or-treating this year?"

"No!" I shook my head. "We're going to the school dance."

"That should be fun." Mrs. Spielini walked over to us.

"Hilary, this is Mrs. Spielini," I said.

"Nice to meet you, Hilary," said Mrs. Spielini.

"Nice to meet you, too," Hilary said politely. "Well, I'll see you tomorrow, Abby. I've got to go."

"Okay." I waved good-bye.

"Seems like a nice girl," Mrs. Spielini commented when Hilary had gone.

"She's my best friend," I replied.

***

I wished I was in the library. In this junior high, dances were held in the afternoon during school hours, so almost everyone could go. Those who didn't want to go to the dance were allowed to study or read in the library under a teacher's supervision until dismissal.

Of course, it was considered pretty nerdy to go to the library, but now it didn't seem like such a bad idea.

I was pinned against the gym wall behind a group of girls from my class, including Sophie and Allyson Mills. Sophie had come as a rabbit, complete with a furry costume, whiskers, and a pocket full of carrots. Allyson was dressed as Cinderella, in an expensive, ballroom-style gown and shoes covered with silver glitter.

The boys had gravitated toward the other end of the gym. There weren't many people dancing, but everyone except me was talking and laughing and seemed to be having a good time.

"Hey, great costume, Abby!" Will Bryant, who was dressed as a vampire, passed me on his way back from the refreshment table. His hands were loaded with pumpkin-shaped cookies, two cupcakes, and a paper cup full of punch.

I smiled briefly and wedged myself further away from the crowd. Where was Hilary, anyway? I scanned the crowd, but saw no sign of her. She had refused to tell me what her costume was because she wanted it to be a surprise, so I had no idea what to look for.

A tap on my shoulder made me jump a foot in the air. "Having fun yet?" a familiar voice asked.

"Hilary?" I said. "Is that you?"

"Yup." She spun around. "Like it?"

Two large cardboard discs covered in gold-foil Christmas paper hung from strings over her shoulders, one over her stomach, one over her back. Underneath she wore her red gymnastics leotard and a pair of white tights. She had tied her hair into six small ponytails and secured them at the root with red and white ribbons, so that they stood out in tufts all over her head. She had painted a red maple leaf on each cheek and the Olympic rings across her forehead.

"I'm an Olympic gold medal for Canada," Hilary announced.

I giggled. She looked so funny. "For what sport?"

"Gymnastics, of course!" Hilary said.

We both began to laugh.

"How come you're standing over here all by yourself?" Hilary asked.

"Well ..."

"Come on!" she grabbed my elbow. "You can't have any fun stuck back here behind everybody."

"Wait!" I protested.

It was too late. Hilary dragged me over to a group of kids I didn't know and began talking to them. Everyone laughed at Hilary's costume and told her it was great. I stayed behind her.

"Oh, I love this song!" Hilary shouted at me above the music. "Come on, let's go dance!"

"Hilary, I can't ask a guy to dance!" I yelled in desperation.

"You don't need to! Everyone just goes and dances with everyone else," Hilary shouted back. She pushed me onto the dance floor, into a crowd of kids. I gulped and began to shuffle my feet to the beat. Hilary was twisting and stomping and bopping behind me like a grasshopper in sneakers.

It seemed like everyone was watching me stumble around on the dance floor. I felt hot and embarrassed, and gradually I edged myself toward the safety of the gym wall.

I watched Hilary enjoying herself. She looked like she was having the time of her life out there. When the song ended, she searched the crowd and gave me an exasperated glance when she saw me with my back to the wall.

"Abby!" she said. "What's the matter?"

"Nothing," I said. "I just felt like watching."

Hilary poked me. "Yeah, right. Come on. I'm dying of thirst." She led the way to the refreshment table and grabbed a cup of punch. I took a cookie and a cupcake.

"Mmm," I said, biting into the cookie. "These are great. Aren't you going to have any?"

Hilary sipped carefully at her punch. "I can't eat that stuff. I'm way too fat as it is."

I looked at her in disbelief. "You're kidding, right?" Hilary qualified as fat the way a sparrow qualified as an elephant.

"No. I told you I have to keep my weight down. I gained a whole pound since last month, and that's bad news."

"A pound isn't much," I said.

"No, but pretty soon it's two, then three, then five, then ten," Hilary said grimly. "I'm not getting any fatter. I already can't fit into last year's jeans."

"Neither can I," I replied. "I grew almost an inch."

Hilary put her paper cup down suddenly. "Let's go. I feel like dancing."

I followed her back toward the now-crowded dance floor, but hung back as Hilary flung herself into the wave of weaving bodies. I watched from the sidelines until Sophie came up to me.

"Having fun?" she asked.

"Yeah, it's okay," I said.

Sophie looked with amusement at the crush of kids, and pointed at Hilary. "Hilary looks like she's having a great time."

I smiled. "She loves this stuff. Nothing ever seems to get her down."

"Yeah," Sophie said. "Not even the flu."

"The flu?" I asked, watching the dance floor.

"Yeah. She threw up in the washroom after lunch today." Sophie poked me. "Make sure she doesn't sneeze on you."

I grinned. "Okay." I waved as Sophie moved off to join some kids from our class.

I looked at Hilary with envy. I was klutzy and shy and boringly normal. She was friendly and funny and had a brilliant future ahead of her. I wished things were as easy for me as they were for her.

8

Hilary Competes

I stood outside the cafeteria door, waiting for Hilary. Now that I had a friend, this school was beginning to feel comfortable. Hilary and I had been eating lunch together every day for the last two weeks.

"Mmmm," Hilary said, as she stopped in front of me. The aroma of melted mozzarella, fresh dough, and tomato-basil sauce drifted out from the cafeteria. "Pizza!"

I looked at her in surprise. "I thought you hated the cafeteria food."

Hilary licked her lips. "I do. But they get their pizza fresh from Luigi's across the street. It's the best."

I sniffed. "It does smell great."

Hilary grinned and began to hurry toward the cafeteria line. "It's the only thing they serve that's good."

I tucked my brown lunch bag under my arm and began to search for any spare change. "How much is it?"

"A dollar a slice." Hilary kept her eyes glued to the front of the line.

Three gum-covered quarters stuck together in my blue jeans pocket, two dimes from my pencil case, and a nickel wedged into my science text for a bookmark made up the total I needed. I tossed my lunch back into my knapsack and handed the cafeteria worker my money.

He looked at the coins with distaste before dropping them in the cash register and giving me a slice of pepperoni and mushroom pizza.

"Mmmm," I said. I took a small bite while I waited for Hilary. It tasted even better than it smelled.

"Let's go find a seat before I drop all this stuff," Hilary said, juggling her wallet, three slices of pizza, a can of pop, and a wad of napkins.

I grabbed the nearest empty table, but Hilary caught me looking at her strangely.

"Once in a while won't kill me," she said, digging into her first slice. "This stuff is irresistible."

In the last two weeks, Hilary had eaten nothing but fruit, raw vegetables, or yoghurt at lunch, and very little of that. I had told her that I didn't think she was eating enough, diet or no diet. That's when I got the full sports nutrition lecture. Vitamins, minerals, calories — you name it, Hilary knew all about it.

So I was pretty surprised when Hilary said she wanted pizza. High calorie, high fat — I didn't think she'd touch it. And three slices? Plus a can of pop?

Hilary wolfed everything down like she hadn't eaten in weeks (which, in my opinion, she pretty much hadn't). I finished my one slice of pizza and then fished out my lunch bag. Peanut butter sandwich, shortbread cookies, two brownies; Mom must have run out of carrot sticks and apples.

I chewed on half of my sandwich, decided I wasn't hungry, and wrapped the rest up.

"Aren't you going to eat the rest of that?" Hilary asked, eyeing the other half of my sandwich.

"No, I'm full," I said. "Do you want it?"

"Sure," she said, taking a huge bite.

"What about your diet? What about calories and all that stuff?" I asked her.

An annoyed look flashed across her face. "It's okay! I know what I'm doing."

I shrugged. "Okay."

Hilary also ate two of my cookies and a brownie when I said I didn't want them.

I crumpled up my lunch bag. "How much do you bet I can get it in the garbage can with one try?"

Hilary didn't answer. She had a funny, preoccupied look on her face.

"Are you all right?" I asked.

Hilary nodded and forced a smile. "Yeah. I'll meet you out at the soccer field, okay? I'm just going to the washroom."

"Do you want me to come with you?"

"No! No, I'm okay," Hilary said abruptly. "I'll see you later." She stood up and hurried out of the cafeteria.

I spent all afternoon worrying about what I'd said to make Hilary mad at me. She never came out to the soccer field after lunch, and I sat on the fence alone.

***

If she was angry, Hilary never mentioned it. I tried a few times to ask her why she didn't come outside after lunch, but she ignored the whole thing and pretended nothing was wrong. I gave up after a while and decided to forget about it.

It didn't seem very important, anyway. Hilary was training hard for the invitational meet, and she scaled her lunches down again until I thought they'd barely support a mouse, never mind a human body. But Hilary wasn't really losing much weight, and in the weeks before the competition her performance in practice was stronger than ever. She even managed to do her double back pike dismount off the beam well enough to convince Pam to let her use it in the competition.

In our class, we moved on to some harder skills and began working on floor, beam, and bar routines. They were simple, compared to the advanced classes, but they definitely required hard work.

Sophie was friendly, and so was her friend Lisa, who was also in my school. We began to hang out together too, but not as much as Hilary and I did.

On the day of the invitational competition, I woke up early. I rolled out of bed and pulled on a pair of jeans and my Briar Park warm-up jacket. Mom and Dad weren't awake yet, so I went downstairs as quietly as possible and poured myself a bowl of cereal and a glass of orange juice.

Sitting at the table, downing my sugar flakes and juice, I began to wonder how Hilary was doing. This was a big competition for her. I glanced at the clock. Seven-twenty.

Sophie and Lisa had asked me to meet them at the host gym so we could watch the competition together. Hilary had to be there to warm up before eight o'clock. I needed to get there a few minutes early. I wanted to give Hilary something for good luck before she performed.

I slurped up the rest of my cereal, yanked on my sneakers, and grabbed a banana from the fruit bowl on the counter. Pam had told all of the gymnasts a hundred times about proper nutrition. I didn't think she'd approve of sugar flakes.

"Dad!" I called softly from the top of the stairs. "Dad, come on! It's time to go."

A muffled moan escaped from behind the bedroom door. I heard my mother snicker. "It's your turn," she said gleefully.

Dad stumbled out into the hall, yawning. He'd pulled on a baseball cap, sweatpants that looked like mice had been chewing them, a fisherman's sweater, sandals, and green wool socks.

I groaned. "Nice outfit, Dad," I said. He blinked blearily at me.

"My plane got in at two AM," he said, wrapping me in a bear hug. "I haven't seen you for ten days, and all you can say is, 'nice outfit, Dad'?" I giggled as he messed up my hair.

Mom waved from her pile of pillows. "Have fun, honey."

"I will." I tugged Dad downstairs and into the car.

The December morning was cold and I shivered in spite of my warm-up jacket underneath my coat. Dad turned on the heater and pulled out into the street.

"Don't worry, Abs. I won't get out of the car and embarrass you." Dad began to look more awake. "Your friends might think your old dad is some kind of fashion idiot."

"Oh, Dad." I made a face at him.

We pulled up in front of the gym, which looked much larger than the Briar Park Club.

"Have fun, kiddo."

"See you later." I jumped out of the car and raced inside. The girls' locker room was at the end of a dim hallway. I pushed the door open and froze.

Someone was throwing up inside one of the toilet cubicles. The sound was unmistakable. I'd been sick enough times myself to know.

"Hilary?" I said softly. "Is that you?"

The toilet flushed. Hilary opened the door, her eyes red and watery, her forehead beaded with sweat.

"Hilary? What's wrong? Are you sick?" I panicked.

She pushed past me and began to rinse her mouth at the sink.

"Should I go get Pam? Should I tell Carlo? You'd better sit down." I stopped as Hilary turned.

"Don't you dare tell anybody!" she said fiercely.

"But —"

"I mean it, Abby." She stared me in the eye. "I'm okay. I'm going to compete. I'm not sick."

"But you …" I stammered, completely confused.

"Really. I'm okay," Hilary smiled uneasily. "I'm fine. It's just nerves."

"Really?" I asked.

"Really." Her voice was firm. "Are you going to come out and watch?"

"Of course." I suddenly remembered why I had come early. "I brought this for you." I pulled a small tissue-wrapped package from my pocket. Hilary unwrapped it slowly.

"Oh!" She began to giggle, and the tension between us melted away. It was a little plastic figurine of a gymnast twisted around the uneven bars. The saying on the base read, "Don't get yourself in a knot!"

"I love it!" Hilary kept giggling.

"It'll remind you not to get stressed out," I said.

Hilary gave me a hug. "Thanks," she whispered.

"Good luck," I whispered back.

Hilary smiled. "See you out there." She adjusted her red leotard, tightened her ponytail and went out the locker-room door.

I followed her, slung my jacket on a bench in the gym, and sat down, lost in thought.

"Hi! Did we miss anything?" Sophie clambered over the gym bags on the benches and slid in beside me, with Lisa right behind her.

"Not much," I answered. That was an understatement. I still wasn't convinced that Hilary wasn't sick, and just pretending to be well so she could compete. I was pretty sure she'd try something like that. But if Hilary had the flu, she might get hurt if she wasn't strong enough to perform. I chewed on my thumbnail and worried.

"Look, they're starting," Lisa whispered.

The three of us sat silently, watching as the first gymnast approached the balance beam. She wasn't from our team.

The judges were seated nearby, and they scrutinized every detail of the girl's performance. She was good, but not as good as Hilary. She faltered on some of her jumps and took a giant step on the landing of her dismount.

It was interesting to watch the gymnasts compete. I found that I recognized a lot of the skills they demonstrated, especially the ones in the floor routines.

Soon it was Hilary's turn on the balance beam. She walked out confidently, with her chin high and her shoulders pulled back. She already looked like a champion.

Hilary used a simple mount, lifting her legs over the beam, so she was sitting on it, one leg extended in front, one bent. Then she pushed with her bent leg and arched her back into a walkover and finished in a scale, which is the gymnastics term for an arabesque.

I could see the concentration in her face as she prepared for her next move. Extending her arms, she threw herself into a powerful back handspring back layout. She seemed to float in the air, suspended by an invisible thread, before landing with both feet firmly on the beam.

Watching Hilary perform was like watching something magical. Everyone around me was murmuring in stupefied approval.

For her third pass, Hilary showed off a slow, controlled front walkover, then stepped immediately into a split leap, did a full turn on one foot, ran a few steps and dove into a round-off back handspring that threw her high for the double back pike dismount. She landed as steady as a rock.

She raised her hands triumphantly. I let out my breath with a whoosh.

"Wow," gasped Sophie.

"Yeah," Lisa said.

"Yeah!" I agreed. Well, there obviously wasn't anything wrong with Hilary. Nobody could be really ill and perform like that.

All of Hilary's routines were perfectly controlled, perfectly executed, and perfectly beautiful. Her vaults were spectacular.

There was no suspense at all about who would win the meet. Pam and Carlo beamed and all the kids from our club cheered when Hilary stepped onto the podium to accept her first-place medal. She beamed at all of us and gave me a bright smile.

I smiled back, but a small, niggling worry kept tugging at my insides.

9

A Horrible Suspicion

"Mom, this is dumb!" I crumpled up another sheet of notebook paper and threw it on the floor. "I can't think of anything to write!"

"Try the encyclopedia," Mom yelled from the family room, where she was pedalling her exercise bike and watching *Canada AM* on TV. "Or the dictionary!"

"Dictionary," I muttered. "This is ridiculous."

It was seven o'clock in the morning. Mom had dragged me out of bed at six-thirty to do some stretching with her before she started her workout, and I (involuntarily) started working on my creative writing contest entry before school.

"Come on, get up!" Mom had bellowed in my ear. "Morning's the best time for the creative juices to get flowing!"

"Not when your brain's asleep!" I'd replied.

But Mom pried me out of bed, hustled me downstairs in the long johns and ratty T-shirt I had slept in, and led me through fifteen minutes of leg, back, neck, and arm stretches, fifty sit-ups and twenty push-ups.

Before I knew it, I was sitting at the kitchen table, still sweating, eating sugar flakes and nibbling on the end of my pencil, while my mother shouted encouragement from her exercycle. Dad was away on another business trip, so I had no one to defend me against this craziness.

"How about an environmental issue?" she bellowed. "Pollution, extinction, overharvesting?"

"I don't even know what those mean," I yelled back.

"What about women's issues? Equal pay for equal work?" Mom hollered.

"I don't work yet!" I said.

"Politics, then." Mom warmed to controversy of any kind.

"Mom!" I stuck my head around the doorway and watched her puff and blow like a steam engine. "That's adult stuff. If I have to write this stupid thing, I want to write about something that's important to kids."

"Well, think of something," Mom said cheerfully. "Day care, for instance. Working mothers versus housewives, next on *Oprah.*"

I groaned. "Never mind, Mom." I went back in the kitchen and wished I was still asleep. The clock read seven-thirty, so I grabbed my books and swallowed the last gulp of orange juice. I ran upstairs to have a quick shower, change into my jeans and a denim shirt, and wrap my hair into a ponytail for school.

Mom stood by the front door, dictionary in hand, as I ran downstairs. She planted a kiss on my cheek and tucked the book under my arm. "Flip through it," she advised. "I've gotten some of my best ideas that way."

I rolled my eyes at her, slid my feet into my sneakers, grabbed my ski jacket, and ran out the door. I waved to Mrs. Spielini, who was looking out her kitchen window, and started down the sidewalk. It usually took me about twenty minutes to get to school, and I was a little early. I leaned against the brick wall of the school and looked at the dictionary in my hand. I let it fall open and glanced at the page.

The first word that hit my eyes was *snow*. "Global warming" was the phrase that flashed in my head, direct from my mother's list of issues.

"Yeah right, Mom," I muttered. I slammed the dictionary shut and let it fall open again. The next word I focused on was *gormless*, which meant foolish, or lacking sense.

"Yes," I agreed out loud. "This is very foolish or lacking sense. Sometimes I wonder about my mother."

But I tried one last time. Don't ask me why. I guess I was desperate for an essay topic. This time, when the dictionary fell open, one word leaped off the page at me. I stared at it for a long time.

Bulimia.

Bulimia nervosa, a disorder in which overeating alternates with self-induced vomiting, fasting, etc.

Vomiting. Overeating. The words burned themselves into my brain. Hilary had thrown up at that competition. She'd said it was nerves, but she'd acted so weird — hardly nervous at all and angry when I wanted to get Pam to help. What if she'd thrown up on purpose? She was practically starving herself at school, but she wasn't losing weight. Suppose she was stuffing herself in secret and then making herself get sick?

Would she really do that to herself, I wondered. Why? Worry tightened the pit of my stomach. Hilary wouldn't do that, I tried to convince myself. She just wouldn't.

At lunch I went straight to the library and grabbed a bunch of books on bulimia and eating disorders and began flipping frantically through them.

All the books said practically the same thing. Bulimia is a serious eating disorder, in which a person uses forced vomiting, laxatives, extreme exercise, and sometimes diet pills to control her weight. Most bulimics weigh close to their normal weight. Most binge, which means stuffing themselves, then throwing up all the food right away. Some don't binge as much as others, but all of them force themselves to get rid of the food in some way, usually by throwing up. Most of the books talked about anorexia nervosa as well. Anorexia is when someone starves herself, sometimes to death.

I slammed the book shut. The sharp thud made the eighth-graders sharing notes at the end of the table look up and glare at me, but I didn't care. Could Hilary really be doing this to herself? I'd only caught her throwing up once, but I'd seen what little amounts of food she usually ate. Plus, there was the time she had eaten all that pizza.

Another thought struck me. Sophie had said that Hilary had the flu at the Halloween dance. She had caught Hilary throwing up after lunch.

That horrible suspicion weighed heavier on my mind. I knew I had to talk to her.

***

I searched all over the school — the cafeteria, the soccer field, and the main washrooms, but there was no sign of Hilary anywhere. I checked my watch. Fifteen minutes until the bell. I needed to find her before then.

I pushed open the door to the tiny girls' washroom beside the Industrial Arts workshop. No one liked to use it because it always smelled of turpentine and sawdust, and the lights didn't work very well. They kept flickering, which was kind of unnerving.

Hilary was scrubbing her hands under the tap. Her warm-up jacket was crumpled on the floor, on top of her books. She turned and gave me a bright smile.

"Hi, Abby!" she said.

I didn't answer right away. Never in my whole life had I confronted a situation like this, and I wasn't sure what to say.

"Are you okay?" Hilary asked. "You look kind of funny."

"Hilary, what are you doing?" I said.

She ripped some paper towels from the dispenser. "Washing my hands."

"No, I mean, what are you doing with your life?" I said. The words just tumbled out.

"Huh?" Hilary gave me a puzzled look.

I took a fresh grip on my courage. "You're making yourself throw up every time you eat more than three mouthfuls of food, aren't you?"

Hilary avoided my stare. "I think I might have a stomach virus or something. I must have picked it up on Saturday at the meet." She looked up and smiled with her lips, but not with her eyes. "Don't worry, Abs. I'll be fine."

"Hilary, listen to me!" I said. "It's not a virus. I'm pretty sure you have something much worse. It's called bulimia, and I just spent the whole lunch hour reading about it —"

"And that makes you an expert, I suppose," Hilary snapped, turning toward the mirror. "Look, Abby, I'm fine, okay?"

I grabbed her shoulder and spun her around. "Hilary, you're my best friend. I'm not just going to ignore the fact that you're making yourself sick. You've got to tell Pam or your parents or somebody who can help you."

"No!" Hilary looked at me with wide-eyed horror. "Abby, no. You don't understand!"

"You've got to go to the doctor. You've been throwing up just about everything you eat. That's not normal, don't you see?"

She shook her head. "I'm fine. I'm not doing anything wrong."

"Hilary, please!" I begged. "Don't keep doing this."

"Abby, you don't know what it's like! I just can't get fat, so sometimes I throw up. It's no big deal."

"It is too a big deal!"

"No, it isn't," Hilary argued. "Abby, listen to me, okay? 'm thirteen. I've only got a few years left to really make it in gymnastics if I'm going to. I need to stay thin. Competing is oo important to me."

"But you don't have to —"

"Yes, I do!" Hilary said fiercely. "I've been gaining too much weight. Sometimes I can't stop snacking, I just can't ontrol myself ..." Her voice took on a pleading note. 'Please, Abby. Don't tell. You don't really understand what t's like."

I faltered. "But Hilary, it's bad for you. The more you make yourself throw up, the harder it is to stop. And you're doing all kinds of horrible things to your insides."

Hilary lifted her chin. "I don't think so, but even if I am, 'll worry about it after I'm finished with gymnastics. Don't ou understand, Abby? This sport is the most important thing n my whole life. It's my future. I have to keep on winning."

I remained silent.

"Please don't tell."

I sighed.

"If you do, I swear, I'll never speak to you again for as ong as I live. You'd wreck everything." Hilary looked angry or a moment, then pleaded again. "Please don't tell. I'm okay. Really, I am."

Inside I was wavering. I was frightened for Hilary, but I also felt petrified at the idea of losing my best friend. I tried not to show how I felt. I sighed again. "Okay. I won't tell. But don't think —"

Hilary interrupted me with a joyful hug. "Thanks, Abby. Thanks a lot. You're a real friend."

10

Right or Wrong?

The carpet surrounding my desk looked like an explosion at a paper recycling plant. Crumpled sheet after crumpled sheet of notepaper landed on the floor after I had crossed out, rewritten, and liquid papered it to death.

I just couldn't concentrate. After that big scene with Hilary, I couldn't think of anything else. What if I had done the wrong thing? I should never have promised to keep my mouth shut. All the books said bulimia was serious.

I never should have promised. Those words spun in my head, and the last thing on my mind was the writing contest. Mom had left me a nag-note on the kitchen table about it. The deadline was tomorrow, and she wanted to see something finished.

Which is why, at four o'clock in the afternoon, I was sitting at my desk amid a litter of notepaper and chewing on the end of my pencil.

"How's it going?" Mom stood in the doorway, with her briefcase in one hand and high heels in the other.

"Fine," I said. "I didn't hear you come in."

"You must have been thinking hard," Mom smiled. "Got that winning entry done yet?"

"No." I felt suddenly irritated. Didn't Mom think of anything but winning? She was just like Hilary. Couldn't she see that there were more important things in life than competing?

"I'm going over to see Mrs. Spielini," I announced defiantly. "I'll work on this later."

"Okay," Mom said. "Be back for supper."

I grabbed a jacket and let the screen door slam behind me as I dashed up to Mrs. Spielini's front porch. Her kitchen light was on, and it sent a comforting glow out into the winter gloom. I wiped my feet on her welcome mat and rang the bell.

"Why, Abby!" Mrs. Spielini opened the door. "I haven't seen you in a long time. Come on in, honey."

I stepped inside and looked glumly at the cheery kitchen. Fresh oatmeal muffins were cooling on a platter, and I could smell lasagna baking in the oven. Mrs. Spielini was wearing the sweatshirt her grandkids had given her for her birthday. It was printed with ladybugs and read, "Don't bug the cook" across the front.

"What's the matter, Abby?" Mrs. Spielini asked. She pulled out a chair at the table and motioned for me to sit down.

I sighed. "Oh, nothing."

"Oh, really. That's funny. Your face is so long, you're nearly stepping on it."

I managed a smile.

"That's better. Now, come on. Tell me about what's bothering you. Has your mother signed you up for a public speaking course?"

"No." I shook my head.

"Well?" Mrs. Spielini prompted.

"Well, suppose you had this friend," I said, "who was doing something that could really hurt her, and you couldn't stop her from doing it."

"What, like knife-swallowing? I'd advise her to give it up pretty quick, if you ask me."

"Suppose she didn't listen to you, though? Suppose she said that knife-swallowing was her whole career, and that if you made her give it up, she'd hate you forever?"

Mrs. Spielini took a deep breath. "What are we really talking about here, Abby?"

"Bulimia," I said. "Do you know what that is?"

Mrs. Spielini looked thoughtful. "I've heard of it."

"It's horrible. It's an eating disorder," I said. "Remember Hilary? My friend from gymnastics? Well, she's so good at the sport, so driven, you wouldn't believe it." I sniffled. "But she says that if I tell anyone about her bulimia, she'll never speak to me again. She says she has to make herself throw up to stay thin, and she won't listen to me when I tell her how dangerous it is. I read a whole bunch of books, and they all described what awful things happen to your body when you do that, and ..." I stopped because my voice was breaking. "I don't want to lose my best friend, but I don't want her to keep doing this to herself. I promised not to tell, but she's going to get really sick. I know she is!"

"Abby," Mrs. Spielini said, touching my shoulder.

I swallowed. "What should I do? If I tell her coach, she'll hate me! But if I don't tell anyone ..." I trailed off.

"What are you going to do?" Mrs. Spielini asked.

"I don't know," I said miserably.

"Does anyone else know about this?"

"I don't think so," I said. "I'm not sure."

"Abby, you know, sometimes a promise is better broken than kept," Mrs. Spielini said. "And some promises you should never be asked to make in the first place."

"What do you mean?"

"I mean sometimes, if keeping a promise means hurting someone instead of helping, then it's not the right thing to do."

I breathed a long, shuddering sigh. "I know. But it's hard."

"Of course it is," Mrs. Spielini's voice was sympathetic. "Hilary hasn't been fair to you. She's asked you for something that is impossible to give."

I watched through the kitchen window as Mom stuck her head out our front door and yelled, "Abby! Dinner!"

"I'd better go," I said.

Mrs. Spielini stood up. "Think about it, Abby. If staying quiet is going to keep you awake at night worrying, it's the wrong decision."

I nodded and ducked out into the snowy dark. The air felt cold on my forehead as I sprinted across the yard and dashed up our front steps.

Mom set a plate of steaming roasted chicken, potatoes, and peas on the table. I slid into my place as she dished out her own plateful and sat down across from me.

"Well, did the break help get your creativity flowing again?" she asked.

"Mmm-hmm." I was thinking about what Mrs. Spielini had said.

"Good. Are you going to show me the final draft?"

"Of what?"

"Of your contest entry, silly." Mom sighed in exasperation. "Honestly, Abby."

"Uh, maybe in the morning," I said. "I'll probably be working on it pretty late." Hah. If I worked on it at all. I couldn't stop worrying about Hilary.

"All right." Satisfied temporarily, Mom turned to the business section of the newspaper, which she never had time to look at in the morning, and began to read.

I stared at the pattern on the wallpaper and tried to think. I shovelled down my dinner, rinsed my plate, and put it in the dishwasher. "I'm going upstairs," I said.

"Mmm-hmm," Mom mumbled. She was engrossed in the stocks pages, which meant a bomb could go off and she probably wouldn't hear it.

I sighed, climbed the stairs to my bedroom and flopped down on the bed. The messy desk and ankle-deep scrunched paper on the floor reminded me again of the writing contest, and of how trivial it seemed compared to what Hilary was dealing with.

I ignored my Language Arts notebook and picked up the pale blue stationery pad I use for a diary, or when I just want to jot down some important ideas. I thought for a minute, then began to write.

What is friendship worth? For some, it means very little. For others, it's everything. For me, it's important enough to be loyal and honest. My friend needs help. No one knows that but me …

When I was finished, I'd covered four and a half sheets of stationery with my thoughts about moving from Edmonton, my friendship with Hilary, and her disease. I questioned whether Hilary was truly my friend. I debated how much our friendship meant to me.

I read over what I had written, and suddenly my decision seemed clearer, more definite. I needed to tell someone about Hilary. I didn't know her parents, but I did know her coach. I decided to tell Pam what was going on. Hilary couldn't go on hurting herself this way, and maybe Pam could help.

My mind was made up. Hilary was my best friend. She was important to me, important enough to help her, even if it meant that we might never be friends again.

11

A Big Decision

B *zzzzzz!* My alarm clock shrilled in my ear and I looked at the time. Seven-thirty already. It felt like I had slept only a few minutes, instead of a few hours. I'd spent the rest of the night copying most of what I'd written about Hilary, reworking it into an essay for the creative writing contest. No one except Hilary would recognize what I was really saying, but the meaning was there.

I rolled out of bed with a groan. If only I could get some more sleep! I threw on some clothes, grabbed two bananas, my lunch, and my homework and headed out the door. I was too nervous to sit down for breakfast, and besides, it was already late.

I peeled a banana as I walked and thought about Hilary. She would be furious when she found out what I was going to do, but I planned to keep it a secret for as long as possible.

Still, I felt guilty. Breaking a promise is not something I would usually do. But Hilary was asking me to do the impossible — sit and watch her ruin her body without doing anything to help. I couldn't do that.

I handed in my five-page essay entry to Mr. Kramer in Language Arts class, which he accepted with a surprised look on his face. I guess he never expected me to enter the contest.

After that, the day dragged. I kept watching the clock, waiting for school to end. I avoided Hilary at lunch because I knew I'd feel bad about pretending everything was the same, when it wasn't.

When the last bell finally rang, I leaped from my seat and bolted for the door. I wanted to catch Pam alone before gymnastics class. I unlocked my locker in record time, snatched my gym bag from the hook, and raced out of the building. My sneakers pounded against the sidewalk and my breath caught painfully in my side. I finally slowed to a walk after about five blocks. The gym wasn't much farther.

I was still puffing when I reached the familiar glass door. I stood outside for a few seconds to catch my breath and rehearse for the fiftieth time what I was going to say.

"Pam," I muttered under my breath, "there's something you should know." I stopped. "No, that sounds too stiff." I tried again. "Pam, I'm kind of worried about Hilary. You see th —"

"Abby!"

I was so startled I clamped my jaw shut and nearly bit my tongue in two.

Pam stood behind me, a large key ring in her hand. "You're early today. Been waiting long?"

I shook my head painfully. My tongue really hurt. "No, but I need to talk to you about something."

"Sure." Pam unlocked the door. "Some problems in class?"

"Not exactly."

"I'll bet you're worried about the beginners' competition next month. Well, don't be. You've got all the skills down perfectly. You've turned out to be one of the best gymnasts in the class, Abby."

"Pam, it's not the competition."

Pam looked at me. "What is it, then?"

I took a deep breath. "It's Hilary."

Pam frowned. "What's the matter with Hilary?"

I bit my lip.

"Come on, Abby. Tell me."

"I don't know any other way to say this," I began, "so I'll just come right out and say it." I exhaled. "Hilary's bulimic."

"She's what?"

"Bulimic. She has bulimia."

Pam inhaled sharply.

"How do you know?"

"I've caught her throwing up right after she's eaten and she didn't have the flu or anything. Most of the time she hardly eats anything at lunch, but sometimes she'll binge." I blinked back sudden tears. "I've read a bunch of books about it. Everything they say about bulimia fits Hilary perfectly."

Pam remained silent.

"I'm really worried about her."

Pam sighed. "I'm sorry to say that this doesn't really surprise me. I've noticed that Hilary has been acting differently for a while. Her performance in practice has been sporadic and she isn't improving as much as she should." She shook her head. "I was beginning to wonder if something like an eating disorder was behind it." She looked me in the eye. "You're absolutely sure, Abby?"

"Yes. She admitted that she made herself throw up to stay thin when I tried to talk to her about it and tell her how stupid she was being."

Pam gave me a weak smile. "I don't suppose that went over very well."

"No." I sniffled. "She said that if I ever told anyone about her throwing up, she'd never speak to me again as long as she lived."

"But here you are," Pam said.

"Yeah, well, I figured I'd rather have Hilary not speak to me for the rest of her very long life than have her as my best friend for a short one."

Pam smiled. "You're a good friend, Abby."

"Hilary won't think so when she finds out I talked to you."

"I won't tell her who told me."

"It won't take her long to figure it out. I'm the only person who knows."

Pam chewed on her lower lip. "That's a tough one."

"I thought about it before I came here." I tried to shrug. "What I want to know is, what are we going to do to help her?"

"For starters, I'll talk to her parents," Pam answered briskly. "Then we'll talk to her and recommend some counselling programs for her."

"She won't go. She doesn't even think there's anything wrong with what she's doing."

"Well, we'll try to convince her." Pam checked her watch. "We'd better get going. It's almost time for class." She smiled. "Thanks for telling me about this, Abby. I hope someday Hilary can appreciate what a caring friend you are."

"Me too," I said, but the words stuck in my throat. I knew that once Hilary found out I had broken my promise, my best friend would be gone for good.

12

Waiting ...

Chewing your fingernails doesn't help when you're nervous. I should know. Every single one of my fingernails was ragged and bitten short, and my stomach was still a tangle of frazzled nerve endings.

It was Friday morning. I was sitting at my desk in Mr. Kramer's homeroom and already dreading lunch period. I'd talked to Pam on Wednesday night. She had said she'd speak to Hilary on Thursday after practice. That was last night.

By now Hilary knew that I had broken my promise. I tried not to think about that.

"Morning everybody," Mr. Kramer called. He strode into the classroom with his usual energy and beamed at us. "Today's the big day!"

The class stared at him blankly. Most of the kids in our class don't wake up until some time after lunch, so no one knew what he was talking about.

"Today's the day the contest finalists are chosen," Mr. Kramer continued. "The list of finalists will be posted after school. I'll be tacking up the sheet of creative writing finalists on my door right after the bell, so good luck to all of you who entered." He gave us all a wink, then began taking attendance.

I paid no attention.

Luckily enough, I managed to get through the whole morning that way. I must have had a preoccupied look on my face, the kind that makes teachers think that a kid has a big problem and isn't just goofing off.

When the bell rang, I dropped my books in my locker and headed for the cafeteria. Hilary was leaning against the doorway, her arms folded across her chest, waiting. I swallowed hard and walked up to her.

"Hi," I said.

Her glare froze me in my tracks. "You told," she said. "You told and you promised you wouldn't. I hate you, Abby." Hilary blinked back tears.

"I had to tell. Don't you understand?" I pleaded. "If someone doesn't help you, you could get really sick."

"I told you already that I know what I'm doing. I thought you were my friend, Abby. I trusted you!" Hilary practically spat out the words. She glowered at me for a moment, then turned and ran down the hall.

"Hilary, wait!" I yelled. But she didn't turn back.

I don't know how long I stood there, students streaming around me and into the cafeteria. I couldn't move. I couldn't think. All I could feel was a heavy, guilty, lonely lump inside my chest. Hilary was gone. She'd never forgive me. I knew it.

"Abby?" The nudge at my elbow startled me. Sophie stared at me in concern. "Are you okay?"

I tried to speak, but only a squeaking noise came out.

Sophie's eyes widened. "What's wrong? Are you sick?"

I shook my head. "No, I'm okay. I just had a ... a fight ... with Hilary. That's all."

"Oh." Sophie looked relieved. "Jeepers, you scared me. I thought you were going to pass out or something."

"No, I'm okay," I repeated.

"Is Hilary really mad?" Sophie asked.

"Yeah. She is."

"How come?"

I was tempted to tell the whole story, but then Hilary's secret would really be out of the bag. I just shrugged.

Sophie didn't press for details. "Well, do you want to eat lunch with Lisa and me?"

I managed a smile. "That's the best offer I've had all day."

***

Mr. Kramer's Language Arts class was my last one of the day. I trooped in with the energy of a burnt-out battery and slumped into my seat. I hadn't stopped worrying about my fight with Hilary all afternoon.

"Okay everybody, settle down," Mr. Kramer said. "I know you're all excited about the creative writing finalists, so I've decided not to keep this class in suspense." He winked. "That's the benefit of having your homeroom teacher as the judge."

Will Bryant ignored Mr. Kramer and busied himself with making faces at Sophie and me.

Sophie frowned at him. "Quit it," she hissed.

I stared out the window.

"Out of our whole school, only five finalists were picked," Mr. Kramer continued.

"We know, we know," muttered Will. He made a pig nose at Sophie and crossed his eyes.

Sophie shot him a murderous look.

"And out of those five, I'm proud to say that the only seventh grade finalist is from this class," Mr. Kramer continued.

Everyone perked up. I barely listened.

"And that finalist is ... Abby Berkowski," Mr. Kramer beamed.

Sophie gasped and squeezed my arm. "Oh, wow!"

I felt like I had been turned to stone. I was a finalist? I had to get up on the auditorium stage and read my essay? In front of the whole school?

"Breathe, Abby," Sophie whispered. "You're turning kind of blue."

I forced my lungs to inhale. I couldn't read my essay. No matter what anyone said, not my mother, not my teacher, not … Hilary. Hilary. I blinked. Hilary wouldn't care any more, anyway. But my essay was about her. I'd written it to show Hilary why I had to break my promise.

"Congratulations, Abby." Mr. Kramer placed my entry on my desk and reached to shake my hand.

I felt numb. "Thank you," I whispered.

Mr. Kramer seemed to understand that I couldn't face all the attention, because he never said another word about the contest. Instead, he made the whole class do grammar worksheets until the bell. Everyone worked hard under the threat that what we didn't get done we had to finish for homework.

I did the worksheets mechanically, handed them in at the bell, and hurried out of classroom. Sophie followed me, chattering.

"Oh, I'm so excited for you," Sophie bubbled. "Want me to help you practise reading out loud? My mom made me take acting lessons last year."

I forced my stiff lips to smile. "Sure," I said.

"Great. How about right now?"

"Okay."

The heavy school doors shut behind us with a thud. Sophie still hovered near my elbow, but I didn't hear a word she said.

A feeling of dread settled into the pit of my stomach. Oh, how I wished I had never written that essay.

13

Backstage Jitters

Hold still, Abby!" Mom doused me with hairspray.

"Mom!" I squirmed impatiently. Sophie watched from where she was perched on the edge of my bed.

"I'm almost done." Mom patted a few hairs into place and surveyed her work. "Very nice," she said.

I looked at myself in the mirror. My hair was french-braided straight down my back and tied with a small red scrunchie. (Mom wanted a ribbon, but I put my foot down.) I was wearing a red plaid skirt that Sophie had lent me, my own denim shirt, and black lace-up oxfords. Sophie had suggested hiking boots, but Mom freaked out.

"You look great," Sophie said, admiring my braid.

"Very impressive," Mom agreed.

I turned away from the mirror and wished the tremors in my knees and stomach would disappear. I looked at my watch.

"It's time to go," I said. My voice sounded strange and hoarse, like I had a sore throat.

Sophie slipped a cough drop into my palm. "You'll be fine," she whispered. "You're wearing my lucky skirt, remember? Besides, we've been practising for days."

That was the truth. Sophie had listened to me read my story out loud every day after school for the last week. It had, in fact, sounded pretty good last night at the kitchen table in front of my mom and dad, Sophie, and Mrs. Spielini.

But now, with my voice all clogged up and my knees sending quivers all the way up my backbone, I wasn't so sure I could do this. The only thing that kept me from backing out was the hope that Hilary would hear me and that maybe it would make her understand.

I popped Sophie's cough drop into my mouth and wheezed as the strong menthol fumes invaded my sinuses.

"Extra strength," Sophie said. "I figured you'd need it."

"Thanks." My eyes were watering.

"Okay everybody, let's move it," Mom yelled. "Mrs. Spielini will be waiting."

Dad folded up his newspaper in the family room and brushed the creases out of his suit. "I've been waiting," he grumbled, "for half an hour." But he smiled proudly at me when I came down the stairs.

We all scrambled into the car, reserving the front seat for Mrs. Spielini. She climbed in carefully and smoothed the skirt of her flowered dress.

"All ready, Abby?" she asked as she fastened her seatbelt.

"No," I said truthfully. Mom nudged me, but Mrs. Spielini smiled.

"You'll do just fine. Trust me."

I don't remember the ride to school, or getting out of the car and walking inside. I must have done it, though, because the next thing I knew, I was backstage. Mom and Dad hugged me for good luck, and Sophie gripped my hand so tightly my fingers grew numb.

"Do you need another cough drop?" she whispered.

I shook my head. "No. One was enough," I said.

"Okay. Good luck!" Sophie followed my parents and Mrs. Spielini down to the auditorium seats, leaving me alone in the dim light backstage.

My whole chest felt tight, like it was encased in iron and I couldn't breathe. I tried to swallow and found that I couldn't. I almost wished I had another of Sophie's cough drops after all.

Mr. Kramer rushed up to me. "Abby! There you are! I've been looking all over for you. Come on up with the rest of the finalists in the stage wings. We're ready to start."

A fresh wave of fear washed over me. I gripped the copy of my essay tightly and thought of Hilary.

"Okay, everybody," Mr. Kramer spoke above the murmur of the crowd beyond the curtains. "Here's your order. Mickey Johnson, Lana Ohlar, Abby Berkowski, Neil Fishbein …"

I leaned weakly against the wall. At least I wasn't first, but I only had about ten more minutes before I had to face that horribly huge audience.

The curtains were pulled back and Mr. Kramer stepped out to the lectern and made a short speech about how difficult it was picking only five finalists. Then he talked about the tremendous talent displayed at Dr. Alfred Sponnick Junior High, and how everybody should be proud to be a part of the talent contest. He introduced the finalists in the writing category, and we each had to walk out on stage as he said our name. Then we had to sit in the five chairs just behind the podium and wait for our turn to read.

I couldn't believe they made us sit out there and stare at the audience. I wished we could have stayed backstage.

Mickey was first up, and he read a funny story about an absent-minded race car driver who drove a cement truck in a race instead of his sports car. Everyone laughed and clapped when Mickey finished.

Lana read a long poem about the change of seasons. It was nice, and every verse rhymed like it was supposed to. Lana received applause, too.

Then it was my turn. Petrified, I rose from my seat and walked stiffy to the centre of the stage. Clutching my essay, I stared out at the audience from behind the lectern. I'd already seen my mom and dad and Mrs. Spielini. Sophie was sitting with Lisa and some other kids from our class. I looked down slightly and saw Hilary staring up at me in amazement from the fourth row.

I took a deep breath. Okay Hilary, this is it, I thought.

"This essay is …" My voice was so small and hoarse I could barely hear it. I cleared my throat and stepped closer to the microphone. "This essay is called 'True Friendship,' " I repeated.

My mouth was so dry, I felt like I'd been sucking on sawdust. I swallowed desperately. "Friendship means different things to different people," I said. "To me, it means being honest."

I looked out at the audience. "For instance, what if a friend's fly is unzipped, and she's about to do a book report in front of the entire class?"

Everyone chuckled. The noise startled me, and I paused until they'd finished.

"Be honest," I said. "Tell her, even if she's embarrassed, because friends don't let each other look stupid." The audience chuckled again and I began to relax a little.

"And what if you're in the middle of the school cafeteria and a friend gets spinach caught between her teeth?" I asked.

This time the audience really laughed. I paused before delivering the next sentence.

"Be honest with her," I said. "Tell her, because friends don't let each other feel dumb."

I stopped and tried to steady my voice. "But suppose a friend is hurting herself, suppose she has a terrible problem, and she won't listen to you." I swallowed, and the audience remained still.

"Be honest. Tell somebody who can help," I said. "Because friends don't let each other suffer, not without a fight."

Absolute silence fell.

The rest of my essay was simple. I read what I had written about the worth of friendship, and what being a friend really means. I said that friendship is a responsibility as well as a joy, that a true friend knows when to be helpful, and when to run for help.

"Friendship isn't just about hanging out at the mall or or goofing off after school. It's about being there when you need each other." I finished.

A hushed stillness enveloped the auditorium. My knees quaked as I stepped away from the support of the lectern.

A sudden crash of applause scared the wits out of me, and I could barely wobble to my seat. Mr. Kramer smiled at me and stepped up to the microphone.

"Ahem," he said, waiting for the applause to stop. "Ahem. Thank you, Abby, for a very powerful piece of writing."

I sank into my chair with relief and smiled in the general direction of the audience. The rest of the program was a blur. Mr. Kramer led us backstage after the readings were over.

"Your essay was terrific," said Lana.

"Yeah," Mickey agreed. "Way to go, Abby."

"Thanks," I said. "But I'm sure glad that's over."

"Me too," Lana said. "I was so nervous!"

"Really?" I asked. "I thought I was the only one who was."

"No way! I was so scared, I thought my knees were going to collapse," Lana said.

That was a new thought. I had never realized that other kids were worried about getting up in front of an audience. I thought it was only me.

The finalists in the other categories performed, and before I knew it, Mr. Kramer was back at the microphone.

"Thank you, everyone, for your fine performances," he said, smiling. "As you know, in each category, one finalist has been chosen today by our judges," he gestured to a cluster of teachers in the front row, "as the winner. So without further delay, may I have the envelopes, please."

Oh brother, I thought, grimacing. Mr. Kramer was taking this master-of-ceremonies thing just a little too seriously.

"All right then. The winner of the creative writing category is …" Mr. Kramer opened the envelope with a flourish of his hand. "… Abby Berkowski!"

I went rigid with shock.

"Abby's essay on friendship will be published in the city's annual collection of student works." Mr. Kramer beckoned for me to come out on stage.

"Congratulations, Abby," he said, shaking my hand.

"Thank you," I choked out. I felt dizzy and elated and stunned all at once. The applause from the audience swelled and Mr. Kramer held on to my elbow to prevent me from escaping off the stage.

"Wait," he whispered, "and smile."

I smiled weakly and looked out across the sea of faces. The bright stage lights felt hot on my face and my legs were shaking.

Mr. Kramer shook my hand again and then waited until I was safely backstage before he went on announcing the winners in the other categories.

I couldn't believe it. I had won? My essay was the best? My whole body tingled with excitement. I stared at the paper in my hands, at the words I had written.

I had read my essay to hundreds of people, something I never thought I could do — and I had won. I was no longer the shy kid! I leaned against the wall for support — my knees felt suddenly unsteady — and a burst of happiness rushed through me.

I really *could* do things. I could get up and talk in front of people, I could do gymnastics, and even do it well. I could make friends, and that was most important of all.

Sophie came charging up to me through the backstage curtains, ignoring the teacher who tried to protest. "Abby, you won!" she shrieked, throwing her arms around my neck. "Oh, I'm so proud! Did my skirt help? It helped, didn't it? I told you it was lucky!"

"Yeah," I said, hugging her. "The skirt helped."

"Come on," she released her grip around my neck and grabbed my arm. "Your parents must be dying to see you. And so's our whole class."

I shrank back for a minute, as some of the old, fearful shyness welled up inside me. But then I took a deep breath and pushed it away. "Okay," I said. "Let's go."

14

Growing Pains

"Abby!" My mother grabbed me and twirled me around, laughing. "I've never been so proud of you in my entire life."

My face was completely scrunched against the buttons of her suit jacket. "Mom, wait," I cried, unplucking a button from my nostril. She paid no attention, but danced with me across the hall. "Mom," I groaned. My whole class had gathered to watch the spectacle, not to mention the rest of the school.

Dad stopped us. "Abs, you were great," he said. I unfastened myself from Mom and he gave me a hug. Mom stood there, grinning like she'd won the lottery. Mrs. Spielini winked at me.

"You were super," she said.

Mr. Kramer came barrelling out from the auditorium and rushed up to me. "Abby, that was terrific. I just wanted to congratulate you again." He lowered his voice. "And don't think I don't know how hard that was for you." He patted my shoulder, then left me to my pride-crazed family, Sophie, and the rest of my class.

I found myself in a cluster of kids. "Hey, Abby! Good job!" Will Bryant said.

"Good job?" Sophie scowled and nudged him with her elbow. "Great job is more like it!"

In the middle of all the confusion, I saw Hilary walking out the auditorium door. I broke away from everyone and hurried up to her.

"Hilary!" I said breathlessly. "Hilary, wait!"

She stopped and regarded me silently. Her face was a mixture of sadness and stubbornness, and suddenly I felt tongue-tied.

"Congratulations on your essay," Hilary said. She gave me a stiff smile.

"Thanks," I whispered. "I wrote it … for you."

Hilary swallowed hard. "I know." She tucked a stray piece of hair behind her ear, and breathed a short, tight sigh. "But you still don't understand." Tears welled up in her eyes. We stared at each other for a moment, then she shrugged and walked off before I could think of anything to say.

I stared after her, gulping down the disappointment that was rising in my throat, and leaned against the wall. Hilary still didn't want to be my friend. All that work, all that practice, getting up on stage, feeling nervous, it was all for nothing. Against my will, two hot tears slid down my cheeks.

"Don't worry, Abby. It'll be okay." Pam came up beside me.

"Pam! I didn't know you were here." I brushed the back of my hand over my eyes. She patted my shoulder.

"I wouldn't miss it, not after Hilary told me you were a finalist."

"Hilary told you?"

Pam nodded. "Abby, she's going through a tough time. I talked to her parents, and we've got her in counselling. I've also told her the truth — that if she doesn't get this eating disorder under control, her gymnastics career will be over within a year." Pam put her arm around my shoulders. "She's under a lot of pressure, Abby. Maybe it's easier for her to be mad at you than mad at herself. But some day, when she realizes what you did for her, you'll be friends again."

"Do you really think so?" I asked.

"I guarantee it," Pam said. "And in the meantime, it looks like you have plenty of other friends to keep you busy." Pam glanced over at my family, classmates, and Mr. Kramer. She grinned, gave me a last squeeze, and disappeared into the crowd.

I felt empty, like I had a deep, hollow spot inside me. Telling Pam about Hilary's eating disorder was the most difficult decision I'd ever had to make. I wished Hilary knew how hard it was for me to lose our friendship.

I looked over at Mrs. Spielini, who was listening patiently to my mother rave about what a great lawyer I would make someday. I looked at my dad, who was talking to Mr. Kramer about the city's annual student publication, and whether or not my essay would make the front page. I looked at Sophie, who was chattering at Lisa, Will, and the rest of my class about how I had borrowed her lucky red plaid skirt.

The hollow ache began to subside a little. I did have a lot of people who cared about me. I'd made friends ... and I had done some things I never believed I could do — participating in gymnastics, winning a writing contest, speaking in front of an audience. In some ways I hardly recognized myself.

And maybe Pam was right. Maybe someday Hilary and I would be best friends again. I really hoped so.